Down on the Farm

Down on

Rita Lascaro

**Green Light Readers
Harcourt, Inc.**

Orlando   Austin   New York
San Diego   Toronto   London

the Farm

I see my dog play.

I can play like my dog.

I see my cat nap.

I can nap like my cat.

I see my hen flap.

I can flap like my hen.

I see my duck swim.

I can swim like my duck.

I see my friends ride.

I can ride like my friends . . .

. . . down on the farm.

FOLLOW THE ANIMALS

How do animals move?
Play animal follow-the-leader with
your friends and find out!

1 Choose an animal.

2 Say the animal follow-the-leader rhyme.

3 Move like the animal.

4 Pick a new leader and play again!

A little **duck** went out to play.
  Back and forth it moved this way.
Come along and follow me,
  A little **duck** is what you'll be!

Quack, quack.

This is a duck.

What Do

Moo-o-o-o.

This is a cow.

Hee-haw,
hee-haw.

This is a donkey.

They Say?

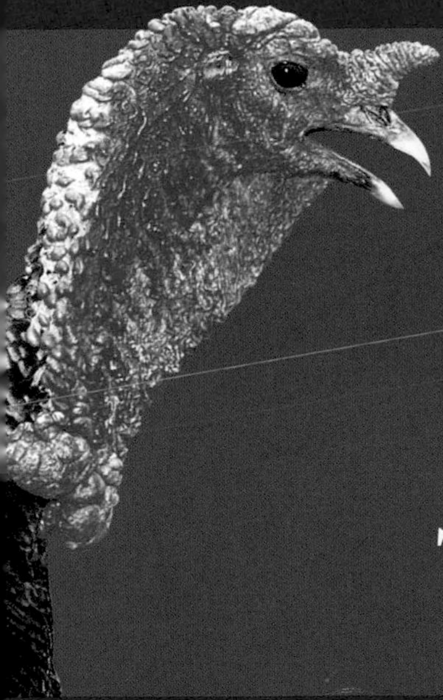

Gobble,
gobble.

This is a turkey.

Can you move like me?

Meet the Author-Illustrator

Rita Lascaro has fun making the pictures for her books. She uses cut and torn paper. At home she has drawers full of paper of many colors, sizes, and textures.

First she draws her pictures. Then she finds just the right paper to glue onto them. She also likes to use hole punchers and scissors to make designs.

Requests for permission to make copies of any part of the work should be mailed
to the following address: Permissions Department, Harcourt, Inc., 6277 Sea Harbor Drive,
Orlando, Florida 32887-6777.

www.HarcourtBooks.com

First Green Light Readers edition 1999
Green Light Readers is a trademark of Harcourt, Inc., registered in the
United States of America and/or other jurisdictions.

The Library of Congress has cataloged an earlier edition as follows:
Lascaro, Rita.
Down on the farm/Rita Lascaro.
p. cm.
"Green Light Readers."
Summary: A child naps like the cat, flaps like the hen,
swims like the duck, and imitates the other animals on the farm.
[1. Domestic animals—Fiction.] I. Title.
PZ7.L3265Do 1999
[E]—dc21   98-15567
ISBN 0-15-204815-4
ISBN 0-15-204855-3 (pb)

A C E G H F D B
A C E G H F D B (pb)

Ages 4-6
Grades: K-1
Guided Reading Level: C
Reading Recovery Level: 4

Green Light Readers
For the reader who's ready to GO!

"A must-have for any family with a beginning reader."—*Boston Sunday Herald*

"You can't go wrong with adding several copies of these terrific books to your beginning-to-read collection."—*School Library Journal*

"A winner for the beginner."—*Booklist*

Five Tips to Help Your Child Become a Great Reader

1. Get involved. Reading aloud to and with your child is just as important as encouraging your child to read independently.

2. Be curious. Ask questions about what your child is reading.

3. Make reading fun. Allow your child to pick books on subjects that interest her or him.

4. Words are everywhere—not just in books. Practice reading signs, packages, and cereal boxes with your child.

5. Set a good example. Make sure your child sees YOU reading.

Why Green Light Readers Is the Best Series for Your New Reader

● Created exclusively for beginning readers by some of the biggest and brightest names in children's books

● Reinforces the reading skills your child is learning in school

● Encourages children to read—and finish—books by themselves

● Offers extra enrichment through fun, age-appropriate activities unique to each story

● Incorporates characteristics of the Reading Recovery program used by educators

● Developed with Harcourt School Publishers and credentialed educational consultants

Daniel's Pet
Alma Flor Ada/G. Brian Karas

Sometimes
Keith Baker

A New Home
Tim Bowers

Rip's Secret Spot
Kristi T. Butler/Joe Cepeda

Cloudy Day Sunny Day
Donald Crews

Rabbit and Turtle Go to School
Lucy Floyd/Christopher Denise

The Tapping Tale
Judy Giglio/Joe Cepeda

The Big, Big Wall
Reginald Howard/Ariane Dewey/
Jose Aruego

What I See
Holly Keller

Down on the Farm
Rita Lascaro

Just Clowning Around: Two Stories
Steven MacDonald/David McPhail

Big Brown Bear
David McPhail

Big Pig and Little Pig
David McPhail

Jack and Rick
David McPhail

Come Here, Tiger!
Alex Moran/Lisa Campbell Ernst

Popcorn
Alex Moran/Betsy Everitt

Sam and Jack: Three Stories
Alex Moran/Tim Bowers

Six Silly Foxes
Alex Moran/Keith Baker

Lost!
Patti Trimble/Daniel Moreton

What Day Is It?
Patti Trimble/Daniel Moreton

Look for more Green Light Readers wherever books are sold!